## The New Adventures of
# MARY-KATE & ASHLEY™

## The Case Of The

# Surfing Secret™

# Look for more great books in

## series:

*The Case Of The Great Elephant Escape*™
*The Case Of The Summer Camp Caper*™

### and coming soon
*The Case Of The Green Ghost*™

# The New Adventures of MARY-KATE & ASHLEY™

# The Case Of The
# Surfing Secret™

by Cathy East Dubowski

**HarperEntertainment**
*A Division of HarperCollinsPublishers*

A PARACHUTE PRESS BOOK

Parachute Publishing, L.L.C.
156 Fifth Avenue
Suite 325
New York, NY 10010

Dualstar Publications
c/o Thorne and Company
1801 Century Park East
Los Angeles, CA 90067

## HarperEntertainment

*A Division of* HarperCollins*Publishers*
10 East 53rd Street, New York, NY 10022-5299

For information, address HarperCollins Publishers,
10 East 53rd Street, New York, NY 10022-5299

ISBN 0-06-106585-4

HarperCollins®, ♣®, and HarperEntertainment™ are trademarks of
HarperCollins Publishers Inc.

First printing: August 1999

Printed in the United States of America

Visit HarperEntertainment on the World Wide Web at
http://www.harpercollins.com

10 9 8 7 6 5 4 3 2 1

# TROUBLE IN THE SUN

**"S**urf's up, dude!" I cried. I slipped on my cool new sunglasses. "Let's go hang ten! The waves are jamming!"

My twin sister, Ashley, gave me a weird look. "What are you talking about, Mary-Kate?"

"I'm practicing my surfer talk. I have to be ready for when I win this cool surfboard." I picked up a flyer from my bed and read it again.

MIRACLE BEACH
SURFING CONTEST
JUNIOR CATEGORY:
AGES FIFTEEN AND UNDER
FIRST PRIZE:
A BRAND-NEW SURFBOARD

The picture showed a boy standing on the beach holding an awesome yellow and green surfboard.

I handed the paper to Ashley. "That board has my name written all over it."

"No way!" Ashley shook her strawberry-blond hair and laughed. "How are you going to get first place? We only know how to surf a little."

I shrugged. "We're on our way to a surfing lesson, right? Maybe it's just what I need to win."

My name is Mary-Kate Olsen. I'm ten years old. Ashley and I are on vacation at Miracle Beach. We're visiting a really cool resort. There's lots to do here. People can sleep in the big fancy hotel. Or they can rent one of the cute little cabins that are all over the place.

We're staying in the hotel part with our parents, our big brother, Trent, and our little sister, Lizzie. Even our dog, Clue, is here.

Clue is a brown and white basset hound. She has long, floppy ears and a cute nose. Clue uses her Super-duper Snooper to help us sniff out clues and solve mysteries.

You see, Ashley and I are detectives. We run the Olsen and Olsen Mystery Agency out of our attic back home. But a mystery can happen anywhere—even on vacation.

There's only one problem. Dogs aren't allowed on the beach. So Clue can't come to our surfing lesson.

Clue wagged her tail and barked. She grabbed her leash with her teeth.

"Sorry, puppy," Ashley said. "Not this time."

"We'll see you at lunchtime." I scratched Clue's ears. "Don't forget your notebook," I told Ashley.

Ashley patted her backpack. "Got it. Do you have your tape recorder?" she asked.

"Of course," I said. Then I checked my backpack. Beach towel. Sunscreen. Water bottle. Oops! No tape recorder. I found it and stuffed it in my bag.

My tape recorder and Ashley's notebook were presents from Great-grandma Olive. She's a detective, too. She told us that good detectives are always prepared. That's why we carry the tape recorder and notebook with us wherever we go.

We hurried out of the room with our backpacks slung over our shoulders.

Outside, we headed down a path toward the beach. We saw a man painting one of the benches that lined the walkway.

"I love the color," Ashley said. "Pink!"

"Me, too," I replied.

The man hung a WET PAINT sign on the bench and started painting the next one.

Ashley and I continued along the path in the sunshine.

It was a beautiful day. People were swimming in a big pool in front of the hotel. The leaves on the palm trees swayed in the breeze. I couldn't wait to hit the beach!

It was the perfect day—until we heard a loud scream.

Ashley and I looked at each other.

"That sounded as if it came from the pool," she said.

"Let's go, Ashley!" I cried. "Someone is in trouble!"

# A Mean Prank

Ashley and I raced toward the pool.

"Help!" a girl yelled. "Save her!"

A large crowd gathered at the edge of the pool.

I gasped. "I think someone's drowning." I stood on my tiptoes. But I couldn't see what was going on. There were too many people around.

Ashley grabbed my hand. "Look!"

We saw a girl with curly blond hair standing near some beach chairs. She looked about six years old. She was wearing a blue swimsuit with the name Megan on it. And she was crying.

"Where's the lifeguard?" someone asked.

The lifeguard sat in his chair and rolled his eyes.

"Why isn't he doing anything?" Ashley asked. She pulled me to the front of the crowd.

I stared into the water. I couldn't see anybody in the pool. All I saw was a small doll, floating near the deep end.

Then I heard a splash. A girl in a purple swimsuit dived into the water. She grabbed the doll and swam to the side of the pool.

Megan held out her arms. "Oh, thank you, Tiffany," she told the swimmer. "You saved my doll!"

Ashley and I laughed. We thought someone was really drowning. Thank goodness we were wrong!

A few people cheered when Tiffany

hopped out of the pool. She smiled and took a bow.

The lifeguard crossed his arms and frowned at Tiffany.

"Why is he mad that Tiffany saved the doll?" Ashley whispered.

"I don't know," I whispered back.

Megan stomped over to the lifeguard. Her blond curls shook as she wagged her little finger at him. "You're a big meanie, Scott!" she said. "Maybe they should make Tiffany the lifeguard."

The crowd laughed. Scott's face turned bright red.

"Hey! It's not my job to save *toys*," he snapped. Then he glared at Tiffany. "The surfing lesson starts on the beach in twenty minutes," he told her. "Be there."

Scott hopped off his chair and strode to the other side of the pool.

"He must be our surfing teacher," Ashley said.

"Come on," I replied. "Let's go meet Tiffany. She's going to be in the class, too."

We hurried over and introduced ourselves.

"Saving Megan's doll was so cool," I told Tiffany.

"But why was the lifeguard so mad about it?" Ashley asked.

Tiffany shook her head. "Scott didn't want to save Megan's doll. I guess he thinks I made him look bad."

"But that's silly," I said.

"It's not just that," she told us. "We're both in the junior surfing contest. We're in the fifteen-and-under category. He's fifteen. But he wants to compete with the older surfers." She giggled. "I think he's afraid I'll beat him. Especially since I have an awesome new surfboard."

"We're signed up for the surfing contest, too!" I said.

"And for surfing lessons with Scott,"

Ashley added. "But we're renting boards."

"Cool! The lessons will be lots of fun," Tiffany said. "Hey, race you to the diving board!"

"No thanks," Ashley said. "It's too high."

I dropped my bag and ran after Tiffany.

Tiffany bounced off the end of the board. She did a double somersault and dived into the water.

"Wow!" I called down from the top of the diving board.

"Excellent dive, darling," a woman called from a beach chair. She wore a white bathing suit and sunglasses.

"Keep it up and you'll win the gold medal next week," the man in the chair next to her said.

"Thanks, Mom! Thanks, Dad," Tiffany called to them.

"Wow. Are you in the Olympics or something?" I asked Tiffany.

Tiffany swam to the ladder and laughed.

"No, I'm only eleven." She climbed out of the water. "I've been swimming since I was five. I've won lots of medals. I'll show them to you sometime."

"Want to see *my* famous dive?" I asked Tiffany.

"Sure," she said.

I took three fast steps to the end of the board. And jumped as hard as I could. "Cannonball!" I cried.

*Splash!*

When I came up out of the water, Tiffany and Ashley were laughing.

We swam until it was time for our lesson. Then we walked down to the beach. Scott and some other students were waiting by a wooden lifeguard chair.

"Why don't we introduce ourselves." Scott pointed to a boy in a short blue wet suit. "You're first."

"Hey, dudes!" the boy said "I'm T.J. I'm ten years old. *And* I'm the next winner of

the surfing contest!" he bragged.

"We'll see about that!" I teased.

"My name is Jennifer," the girl beside T.J. said shyly. She had on a swimsuit with a ruffly skirt. "I'm ten, too. But I don't know how to surf at all."

Then Tiffany, Ashley, and I introduced ourselves.

"Okay," Scott said. "Let's go to the Board Room."

Jennifer giggled. "Okay, Scott," she said with a grin.

The Board Room was a place to rent surfboards. It was right on the beach. Hotel guests could store their own boards there, too. A snack bar was next door.

Jennifer giggled again at something Scott said.

*Why is she laughing so much?* I wondered. *Scott isn't* that *funny.*

Then I figured it out. I dug my elbow into Ashley's side.

"Ow! Mary-Kate! What is it?" Ashley demanded.

"Look at Jennifer," I whispered. "She *likes* Scott!"

Ashley and I glanced at Jennifer. She was staring at Scott with a goofy smile on her face.

"I think you're right," she whispered. "Yuck!"

"Here we are." Scott opened the locked door, and we crowded into the room. He pulled the little chain that switched on an overhead lightbulb.

"I can't wait for you to see my new board," Tiffany told us. "It's so cool. It's bright purple with sparkles all over it. My parents bought it just for this trip. It was really expensive."

"Hey, look at this one," I said, pointing to a short black board with orange flames on it. "Isn't it cool?"

Ashley opened her mouth to answer.

But then Tiffany's cry filled the room. "Oh, no!"

Ashley and I spun around—and gasped at what we saw.

Someone had poured thick pink paint all over Tiffany's brand-new surfboard!

# 3

# TWINS ON THE CASE

"**M**y surfboard!" Tiffany exclaimed. "It's ruined! Now I can't go surfing!"

"Dude!" T.J. said. "Someone totally wrecked it on purpose. That's creepy!"

"Wait!" I touched the board with my fingertip. Then I held it up for Ashley to see. "The paint is still wet," I announced. "I bet this just happened."

"Don't worry," Ashley told Tiffany. "We'll find out who did this!"

"So, what are you?" Scott asked with a

snicker. "Detectives or something?"

Ashley and I grinned at each other.

"As a matter of fact…," Ashley began.

"We are," I finished.

Tiffany squinted at us. "Now I know why you two look so familiar. You're the Trenchcoat Twins, right? I read about you in *Kool Kidz* magazine." Tiffany shook her head. "But I can't ask you guys to help. You're on vacation. You're not supposed to be working."

"No problem," I said. "The Olsen and Olsen Mystery Agency never closes."

"That's right," Ashley added. "The Trenchcoat Twins are on the case!"

"Isn't it a little hot for trenchcoats?" Scott asked with another snicker.

I took out my tape recorder and clicked it on.

Ashley pulled out her detective notebook and a pencil. "Okay," she said. "What do you think happened?"

"*Somebody* is trying to stop me from taking lessons. So I won't win the surfing contest!" Tiffany stared at Scott.

Scott rolled his eyes. "Forget it, will you? Maybe it was a joke. Or an accident." He wiped the board with his hand. Pink paint easily came off on his fingertips. "See? It will wash right off. No big deal."

"Are you kidding?" Tiffany exclaimed. "My board is totally ruined! I'll never be able to surf with this."

"Well, you're holding up the lesson with all your complaining," Scott grumbled.

I wanted to ask Tiffany how long her surfboard was in the Board Room. But then Jennifer groaned. She crossed her arms over her stomach.

I clicked off my tape recorder. "What's wrong?"

"I have a really bad stomachache all of a sudden," Jennifer said. "Can we have our lesson later?"

Scott looked as if he was about to blow up. "You're all a bunch of babies!" he yelled. "Why am I teaching little kids, anyway? Today's lesson is canceled!"

"But, dude!" T.J. protested. "I need the practice for the contest!"

Scott pointed to the ocean. "See the waves? Go practice." Then he told the group, "Surfing lessons here. Tomorrow. Nine A.M. sharp. Show up—*if* you're ready for a serious lesson." Then he strode off toward the hotel without another word.

"Scott, wait!" Jennifer cried, and ran after him.

"I thought she had a stomachache!" I said to Ashley. "How come she's running?"

"Forget about Jennifer," Ashley whispered. "Look!"

She pointed at Scott as he walked away. The bottom of his white T-shirt was smudged with something pink.

"That looks like paint," I said. "Mystery

solved. Case closed. Come on, Ashley. Let's go get him!"

Ashley grabbed my arm and stopped me. "Hold on a minute," she said. "You're doing it again, Mary-Kate."

"Doing what?"

"Jumping to conclusions," Ashley pointed out. "Remember what Great-grandma Olive always says? 'Just because something *seems* true doesn't mean it *is* true.'"

"But Scott did it," I insisted. "He's mad at Tiffany. She embarrassed him in front of all those people."

"True," Ashley agreed.

"And he kept trying to tell Tiffany the paint on her board was a joke. He seemed sure it would wash off, too. That could mean he knew what kind of paint was used."

"That does seem suspicious." Ashley scribbled something in her notebook.

"See?" I said.

"But it doesn't *prove* that he did it," Ashley added.

I didn't know what to say next. Ashley had a point. I guess that's why we make a super detective team.

I like to work on hunches. I always want to jump right in. Ashley always thinks things through.

We're like peanut butter and jelly. We're better when you put us together.

"Okay, okay," I admitted to Ashley. "I guess you're right. But I still think Scott ruined Tiffany's surfboard. We just have to find a way to prove it."

"You got it, Mary-Kate!" Ashley said. She slapped me a high five. "Let's get to work!"

# SURFING FOR CLUES

"**Y**ou need a disguise," I told Ashley the next morning.

I stuffed my hair into a cap. Then I slipped on my shades.

"How about this?" Ashley put on Mom's wide-brimmed straw hat and sunglasses. She pulled on her backpack.

"Perfect," I said. "We look just like tourists. Scott will never know we're spying on him." I grabbed my bag. "Come on!"

I was the one who came up with the

idea. First we'd find Scott. Then we'd follow him around until it was time for our surfing lesson.

But finding him wasn't easy. I thought he would be working by the pool. But the pool wasn't open yet. It was too early.

Then Ashley spotted him walking down the path toward a group of cabins. We hid behind palm trees along the way. We saw him pin a piece of paper to a bulletin board.

Next he unlocked the video game room off the main lobby of the hotel. We sat in big overstuffed chairs and pretended to read the newspaper.

Finally he went to the beach and opened the shutters to the snack bar. We ducked behind a huge trash can.

"See that?" I whispered. On the counter of the snack bar was a paint can—with pink drips down the sides.

"That's probably the same paint that ruined Tiffany's surfboard," I said. "And

Scott has the key to the snack bar where it was left." I pumped the air with my fist. "Proof!"

"Maybe," Ashley said.

"*Maybe?*" I asked. "Come on, Ashley, how could this *not* be the proof we need?"

"Don't you remember?" Ashley asked. "We saw a man painting some benches with the same color." She pointed to a pink bench by the pool house. "Remember how he put up a WET PAINT sign? Maybe Scott accidentally sat on a bench that wasn't dry. Maybe that's how he got pink paint on the bottom of his T-shirt."

"But, Ashley," I started to argue. Then I stopped. My twin sister was right. "Okay, so it's not total proof. But it's still very weird."

I sighed. It was time for our surfing lesson to begin. But that didn't mean we should stop working on the case. I decided to keep one eye on my surfboard and the other eye on our suspect.

Everyone met at the Board Room to get their surfing stuff. Ashley and I took off our disguises. We stuffed them in our backpacks. Then we chose our boards. I was picking out a baby blue board, when Tiffany screamed.

"Not again…," Scott muttered.

Ashley and I rushed to her side.

Tiffany trembled as she showed us her surfboard. Yesterday's pink paint had been washed away. But now there was something even worse on it.

A warning was written in black marker: TIFANY—STAY OUT OF THE WATER—OR ELSE!

# OUR SUSPECT CAN'T SPELL

I felt sorry for Tiffany. She looked really scared.

Ashley put her arm around Tiffany's shoulders.

"Who would write this to me?" Tiffany cried. She glared at Scott. "Do you still think this is a joke?"

Scott shrugged his shoulders. He didn't seem too worried.

Tiffany turned to me and Ashley. "You have to solve this mystery soon," she said.

"My parents are coming to watch me surf later this morning. They're going to be really worried. I bet they won't even let me enter the contest. Something bad will happen if I do!"

"You're probably right," T.J. said. "I wouldn't enter if I were you, dude."

*Hmm. T.J. is telling her not to surf,* I thought. *We know he wants to win the contest. Could he have written the note?*

Ashley was still staring at the words on Tiffany's board.

"What is it?" I asked her.

"Mary-Kate," she said, "do you see something strange about this note?"

I stared at the crooked letters written across the board. "Well, the handwriting is pretty sloppy. Is that what you mean?"

"Well, that, too," she said. "But look."

I read the note again: TIFANY—STAY OUT OF THE WATER—OR ELSE!

Then I saw it—as plain as the nose on

my face! "Oh, right," I said.

"Tiffany," I asked. "Do you spell your name with one *F* or two?"

Tiffany frowned. "Two, of course. T-I-F-F-A-N-Y."

Ashley pointed at the surfboard. "T-I-F-A-N-Y," she said. "The person who wrote this note spelled your name wrong. He or she spelled it with only one *F*."

I wasn't surprised that Ashley caught that clue first. She's a really good speller. I always ask her to help me study for spelling tests.

"Whoever did this is a bad speller," I whispered to my sister. "How do we get samples of our suspect's handwriting?"

Ashley grinned. "Simple." She pulled her notebook and pencil out from her backpack. She opened the book to a fresh page and took it to Scott. "Would you sign this—in honor of our first lesson?" she asked him.

Scott snorted. He snatched the notebook and pen out of her hands. "*If* we ever *have* a first lesson…" He quickly scribbled his name.

*Is he always this grouchy?* I wondered. *Or just when Tiffany is around?*

"I'd better report what happened to the manager," Scott said. "Meet me by the shore with your boards. I'll be right back."

That gave us a chance to get the others to sign Ashley's book, too. Then we went outside and sat in the sand. Everyone else took their surfboards to the water. But we stayed behind to study the handwriting.

I was excited. We were about to solve the mystery!

As we flipped through the pages, my heart sank. "Oh, no." I sighed.

"What's wrong?" Ashley asked.

"None of the handwriting matches the writing on Tiffany's board!" I pointed out.

Ashley shook her head. "You're right.

Maybe it's because writing great big letters on a surfboard is a lot different from signing your name."

"I guess," I muttered. "And the suspect could have disguised his or her handwriting," I added.

"Good point, Mary-Kate," Ashley said. "Then let's look for bad spellers."

First we checked T.J.'s note. He wrote: "To Mary-Kate and Ashley, Surf's Up, Dudes! Sincerely, T.J."

I giggled. Did T.J. call *everybody* dude? Even his mom and dad?

"T.J. spelled everything correctly," Ashley said.

I turned the page. Tiffany signed her name with fat curly letters and dotted her *I*'s with tiny hearts. "To Mary-Kate and Ashley, you girls are awesome! Thanks for all your help. Your friend, Tiffany." No misspelled words there.

Jennifer wrote: "Mary Kate and Ashely,

Serfing is cool—and so are you two datectives. Your freind, Jennifer."

"Aha!" I said. "Jennifer is a terrible speller. She's guilty!"

"Maybe," Ashley said.

I shook my head. Maybe, maybe, maybe!

"Let's go get our surfboards," I told Ashley.

"Why would Jennifer write a mean note to Tiffany?" Ashley asked when we went back into the Board Room.

"I don't know," I said. "But we'd better find out quick. Look at this!"

I pointed to a note that was taped to my backpack: TRENCHCOAT TWINS—STOP YOUR SNOOPING OR YOUR SURFING DAYS WILL BE OVER—FOREVER!

# 6

# TROUBLE POPS UP

**A**shley slipped her hand into mine and squeezed it. I squeezed back. This was really creepy.

"Someone must have written this while we were outside looking at my notebook," Ashley said.

I studied the note. "I wonder if we should forget about Jennifer as a suspect."

"How come?" she asked.

"Look! Not a single word is misspelled," I pointed out.

"True," Ashley said. "But I wouldn't cross her off yet."

Before I could ask Ashley why, Scott came into the Board Room. "Let's go to the water," he said.

We joined the rest of the group.

"Okay, gang. Let's see if we can actually have our surfing lesson this morning," Scott announced. "If that's okay with Tiffany?"

Tiffany smiled weakly. She didn't say a word.

We went down to the shore. We watched the waves crash into the sand. The waves were higher than yesterday.

"The wind is picking up," Scott said. "There's a storm offshore. It's really helping the waves."

Tiffany was waxing a rental board. She wore a bright purple wet suit. *She must really like that color*, I thought.

T.J. came up to me and Ashley. He

looked at me over the top of his sunglasses. "Which twin are you?" he asked with a smile.

I grinned. "Guess," I said.

"I would say you're Mary-Kate, right?" he said.

"Not bad," Ashley said.

Then his look got serious. "So you guys are dropping the case, huh?"

"No way," Ashley said. "Why would you think that?"

"Well, I saw the note on your backpack," T.J. replied. "Aren't you scared? I sure would be."

"Nope," I said. *Well, maybe a little*, I thought.

"That note just makes us want to solve the case even more," Ashley added.

T.J. looked surprised. *I guess he believed we would be more frightened*, I thought. Then I remembered something else.

"Isn't it weird that T.J. didn't show us the

note as soon as he saw it?" I whispered to Ashley.

"That seems very suspicious," Ashley whispered back.

We had to stop talking about the case. Scott was ready to start the class.

First we practiced standing on our surfboards in the sand.

"Okay," Scott said after a few minutes. "Now you're ready to try some pop-ups. Everybody lie on your stomachs on your boards."

We all did what Scott said. Then we pretended we were paddling out into the water. When Scott gave the signal, we crouched, and stood up. It seemed kind of funny at first. But Scott said it was the best way to learn before trying it on real waves.

T.J. sang old surfer songs and showed off on his board. He made me laugh.

Jennifer was having trouble. She kept asking Scott to come over and help her.

Tiffany wasn't doing pop-ups at all.

Scott put his hands on his hips. "What's the problem, Tiffany?" he asked with a frown.

"I'm skipping this part," she told him. "It's too easy. It's for beginners."

"Look, Tiffany, I'm the teacher," Scott said. "You want to take lessons? You do what I say, just like everyone else in the class."

"But I'm a champion swimmer," Tiffany said. "I shouldn't even be in this class. I'm better than you. And I've got the medals to prove it."

"Oh, yeah?" Scott said. "I don't care if you've got a hundred little medals. Just wait till the contest. Then we'll see who's the best surfer."

Tiffany folded her arms. "I can't believe my parents made me take this dumb class," she complained.

"Yeah, well, I can't believe I've got to

*teach* this dumb class," Scott muttered under his breath. "And I can't believe I have to surf against little kids."

"I'm not a little kid," Tiffany shot back.

Jennifer and T.J. stopped to watch them fight.

"Scott and Tiffany really don't like each other," I whispered to Ashley.

"Yeah," Ashley agreed. She lay down on her board.

"Not doing any more pop-ups?" I asked.

Ashley crossed her arms on the board and put her head down. "I'm too pooped to pop-up anymore."

I sat up cross-legged on my board and looked at the beach. It was a bright, sunny day. Colorful beach umbrellas dotted the shore. I saw people playing Frisbee and flying kites. Everyone seemed to be having fun.

Then I spotted two grown-ups heading toward our group. But they were too

dressed up for the beach. The man had on blue pants and a blue short-sleeved sports shirt. The woman wore a pretty yellow sundress and sandals. They looked a little familiar.

"Mom, Dad!" I heard Tiffany call out. She ran to greet them. I heard her tell them all about the surfboard and the note.

Her mother hugged her. Her father told her not to worry. "It's just someone who's jealous of you," he said. "People used to play all sorts of tricks on me back in my surfing days. Don't let it scare you."

"Just keep your mind on your goal," Tiffany's mother said. Then she hugged her daughter again. "Oooh, I can't wait to see my little girl take another first prize!"

"She's just like her dad," her father added. "A champion surfer." He hugged Tiffany and laughed. "I think it runs in the family, you know."

Tiffany scowled. I wondered if she was

angry that her parents weren't more upset.

Tiffany's dad looked at his watch. "Is your class starting soon?" he asked. "I managed to slip away from my meeting for a while. But I've got another important meeting in half an hour."

"But I'll be here for the rest of your lesson," her mom told her.

Sometimes companies hold big meetings at hotels. *Tiffany's dad must be an important businessman*, I thought.

Tiffany's parents unfolded a blanket and sat down to watch.

"Okay, guys," Scott called out. "Let's try some of this stuff out in the water."

I dragged my surfboard closer to the ocean. Then I stuck my toe in the water. It was cool—perfect for a hot day.

Ashley kicked some sea foam at me. "It looks like the time you put too much soap powder in the washing machine!"

We waded out till the water reached our

waists. Then we hopped on our boards and paddled out.

For the first time, I actually felt nervous. Was it because of the waves? They were definitely the biggest I'd seen so far this trip. Or maybe it was that scary note.

T.J. paddled up beside us. He started singing some scary music—the kind of music they always play in movies when a shark is about to attack.

"Stop!" I said, laughing. "You're giving me the creeps!"

"Shark!" Ashley screamed.

Yeah, right. "Ha, ha, Ashley," I said. "Very funny."

But Ashley wasn't laughing.

And then I saw it.

A shark fin was slicing through the water.

Heading straight for me!

# 7

# SHARK!

**N**o. *Wait. I'm wrong*, I thought.

I stared as the gray fin moved through the water.

The shark wasn't swimming toward *me* at all.

It was headed straight for Tiffany!

"Tiffany!" I cried. "Look out!"

"Swim!" Ashley screamed.

We all paddled like crazy for the shore.

At last Ashley and I splashed onto the warm sand. We saw Tiffany run out of the

ocean. Her parents stood at the edge of the water. Sobbing, Tiffany threw herself into their arms.

I was so scared I couldn't speak. My heart pounded. My knees began to shake. My—

"Hey, wait a minute." I peered back at the sea.

"W-what is it, Mary-Kate?" Ashley asked nervously.

"Something *really* weird is going on here," I announced. "That shark fin just fell over."

"Huh?"

"See?" I said, pointing. "There's not even a shark attached to it. It's just—"

"A toy!" we both cried at once.

Then I spotted something else. A kid in a rubber raft. His spiky red hair made him easy to see against the pale blue sky. He had a remote control in his hands. He was aiming it at the toy shark fin!

"Do you see what I see?" I asked Ashley.

The boy used his remote to quickly zoom the fin toward him. He pulled it into his raft and started to paddle away.

"Who is he?" Ashley asked. "And why is he trying to scare Tiffany?"

"I don't know," I replied, "but he's getting away. After him!"

We paddled out into the waves on our surfboards. Sea water sprayed into our faces. The waves pounded our boards as we chased the boy.

The noise of the waves drowned out almost every other sound.

Except one.

"*Ahhhhh!*" Ashley cried out.

I looked up.

Uh-oh. We were about to be crunched by the biggest wave I'd ever seen!

# 8

# RIDING THE WAVE

I stared at the foaming, curling wave. It looked like the kind of wave that ate surfboards for breakfast!

I could think of only one thing to do.

"Ashley! Turn your board around!" I shouted at the top of my lungs.

We managed to flip our boards so they faced the shore—just as the monster wave hit us.

"Hang ten!" Ashley shouted.

Ten? "Hang *twenty!*" I yelled. I pressed

all ten fingers and all ten toes into my board.

Then I braced myself for a huge wipe-out.

But that didn't happen. Suddenly I felt myself lifted into the air.

Instead of getting crunched, I was *riding* the monster wave!

I glanced over. Ashley was surfing high on the wave, too!

It felt as if we were going ninety miles an hour!

"Please let us make it to the shore. *Please* let us make it to the shore...," I begged over and over. I hung on with all my strength. I squeezed my eyes shut.

Finally the wave crashed onto the sand. Then I glided through the shallow water. And came to a stop at the water's edge.

I opened my eyes. Whew! Thank goodness Ashley was right beside me.

We lay there a minute, panting.

# ⇐The New Adventures of⇒ MARY-KATE&ASHLEY ™

## DETECTIVE TRICK

### O, WHAT A LIAR!

**Here's a cool way to tell if someone is lying to you:**

Get a sample of the person's handwriting. Make sure the sample has some O's in it! Script is best, but printed letters are okay, too.

Look at the way the person writes the letter O. Honest people usually make an empty, round O. But people who lie often make lots of loops inside their O's, like this:

The bigger the loops inside the O, the more likely it is that the person is a liar!

*From*
**The Case Of The Surfing Secret**

---

# ⇐The New Adventures of⇒ MARY-KATE&ASHLEY ™

## DETECTIVE TRICK

### REBUS CODE

Here's a super-secret code that takes a little creativity! All you need is some paper, a pencil, and your imagination!

First pick your message:
**COME TO A STAKEOUT!**

Then, translate your message into pictures, like this:

Send it to a friend. Your message will look just like doodles!

*Look for our next mystery…*
**The Case Of The Green Ghost**

Then Ashley jumped to her feet, grinning. "All *riiiiiight!*" she cried. "That was so much fun! Let's do it again!"

I sat up, and shoved the wet hair out of my face. *That was really fun. But did that big wave knock Ashley's brains out?* I wondered.

"Aren't you forgetting something?" I asked her.

"Oh, yeah," she said with a weak smile. "Shark-boy."

We glanced around the beach.

"There he is!" Ashley cried. "Near the big yellow umbrella!"

The tall redheaded boy had dragged his raft onto the sand several yards down the beach.

Ashley and I left our boards where they were and dashed toward him.

"Why did he try to scare Tiffany?" Ashley asked as we ran. "I've never even seen him around here before."

"Maybe he's in the contest, too," I suggested. "Besides, that doesn't matter. We *saw* him chase Tiffany with that shark fin. We don't need any more proof than that."

Ashley and I skidded to a stop right in front of him.

He sat there with the shark fin lying in the sand right at his feet.

"Are you the one who was using that toy out there?" Ashley asked.

"Yeah, that was me," he said with a shrug.

*All right! Ashley's probably thinking the same thing I am*, I thought. *We captured our suspect! We solved the mystery. Let's go surfing!*

"We have a few questions for you," Ashley said.

*Okay, maybe we weren't thinking the same thing*, I said to myself.

"What's your name?" Ashley asked first.

"Jazz," the redheaded boy answered.

"What?" Ashley and I asked at the same time.

The boy shrugged. "Well, my real name is Henry. How boring is that? All my friends call me Jazz."

"Okay, Jazz," I said. "Why did you write that note? And what do you have against Tiffany?"

"Yeah, why are you trying to scare her?" Ashley demanded.

Jazz frowned. "What note? And who's Tiffany? I don't know any Tiffany."

Ashley and I looked at each other. This time I *knew* we were thinking exactly the same thing.

*Huh?*

# 9

# SHARK-BOY GIVES US A CLUE!

"**W**ait just a minute," Ashley said. She folded her arms. She stared into Jazz's eyes. "Don't tell us you didn't write that note we found," she said.

"What note?" Jazz asked.

"Don't play dumb," I told him. I tried to sound as tough as Ashley. "The note you wrote in black marker all over Tiffany's brand-new surfboard!" I reminded him. "The one that said, 'Stay out of the water—or else!'"

Jazz's eyes opened wide. "I never wrote a note like that," he said.

"Oh, yeah?" I said.

"Oh, yeah?" Ashley asked, too.

"Yeah," Jazz replied. "I didn't touch anybody's surfboard. I wouldn't do that—it's so lame."

Ashley and I looked at each other. Now what?

"Are you trying to keep Tiffany out of the surfing contest—so you can win?" I asked him.

"Surfing contest?" Jazz asked. "I don't even know how to surf. And I *don't* know any girl named Tiffany."

Was he telling the truth? Or was he just a good liar?

"Then why were you trying to scare Tiffany with your toy shark?" I demanded.

Jazz raked his hand through his spiky red hair. "I guess it was a dumb thing to do. But I was swimming in the ocean this

morning. And when I came out to dry off, I found a note taped to my raft."

"A note!" I glanced at Ashley. "Maybe the same person who wrote the other notes wrote this one, too," I whispered to her.

"Do you still have the note?" Ashley asked the boy.

He nodded and reached for a duffel bag. He pulled out a crumpled sheet of paper and handed it to Ashley.

She carefully smoothed it out. Then we both read it: WANT TO MAKE $10.00? MAKE THIS SHARK SWIM AROUND A BLOND GIRL IN A BRIGHT PURPLE WET SUIT AT 10:00 A.M. IF YOU DO IT, I'LL GIVE YOU THE MONEY. LOOK FOR IT TONIGHT AT 9:00 BEHIND THE EAT-HERE HUT.

The note wasn't signed.

Jazz shrugged. "I know it's kind of weird. But I thought, why not? It's a lot of money! I figured some kid was just playing a joke on his friend or something."

"Hmmm. All the words are spelled cor-

rectly in this note," Ashley pointed out.

"Yeah," I said. "But I think the handwriting is the same as on the note *we* got."

Ashley nodded. "I think you're right. We'll have to check it later to make sure."

"So…am I in some kind of trouble?" Jazz asked nervously.

"No," Ashley told him.

"But that was a pretty mean thing to do," I pointed out. "It scared us, too."

"Sorry," he mumbled. A pink blush spread across his freckled cheeks. "So, uh, what do I do with this?" He held up the fake shark fin. "Should I give it to you?"

"No way!" we both shouted at once. "We've seen enough sharks for one day!"

Ashley and I headed back to our group. "Are we *ever* going to solve this mystery?" I complained.

"Well, Scott is still a suspect because of the pink paint," Ashley reminded me. "And he doesn't like Tiffany. *And* he doesn't want

her to enter the contest."

"I guess T.J.'s a suspect," I said. "He keeps saying Tiffany should be scared by all these notes. And he really wants to win that surfboard," I added. "Tiffany is definitely in his way."

Ashley sighed. "But we're no closer to solving the case than we were yesterday."

"This mystery isn't as easy to solve as I thought it was going to be." I glanced at the note Jazz had given us. "Wait a minute!" I said. "Jazz scared Tiffany with the shark. But he still hasn't gotten paid."

"So?" Ashley said. "What's that got to do with us?"

I grinned. "Whoever is playing these tricks will be at the Eat-Here Hut at nine o'clock tonight to pay Jazz."

Ashley smiled, too. "And *we'll* be there to catch our suspect!"

# A SURPRISE SUSPECT

"**W**-w-what's that?" Ashley whispered as we walked along the path. She grabbed my hand tight.

"Ow! Let go!" I whispered back. "I didn't hear anything."

It was eight-thirty and getting dark. The hotel lights glowed through the tall palm trees. They cast scary shadows on the walkway.

I gulped.

*Snuffle-snuffle. Snuffle-snuffle.*

"Th-there it is again!" Ashley cried.

Ashley was right. Something was making a weird noise. I listened closely to the sound.

*Snuffle-snuffle. Snuffle-snuffle.*

Then I rolled my eyes. "Ashley, that's just Clue sniffing for clues!"

Ashley let out a big sigh of relief. "Oh."

Clue was our reason for being out this late. Mom and Dad let us take her out for a walk. But we weren't walking Clue just anywhere. We were walking her toward the Eat-Here Hut.

With Clue's leash in my hand, Ashley and I crept down the dark path. I thought about that creepy note someone had sent us: TRENCHCOAT TWINS! STOP YOUR SNOOPING OR YOUR SURFING DAYS WILL BE OVER—FOREVER!

I shivered. I was glad we had good old Clue along for protection.

We huddled together and shuffled a few more steps. Ashley and I kept our eyes peeled. Clue kept her nose to the ground.

Then Ashley stopped me. "Wait," she whispered. She stared into the shadows.

I followed her gaze. Then I saw it, too.

Somebody was out there. Somebody carrying a surfboard!

"Let's hide," I whispered to Ashley.

But it was too late.

Clue barked and barked. She pulled on her leash.

Oh, no! Clue was a super detective. But sometimes she didn't know when to keep her muzzle zipped!

The person looked our way. Then the surfboard clattered to the ground. And the person ran away.

We raced toward the board.

"Did you see who it was?" I asked Ashley.

"No," she said. "Did you?"

I shook my head. When we reached the surfboard we bent down to get a closer

look. It was a purple and gold surfboard with sparkles all over it.

Ashley and I both gasped.

Tiffany's surfboard!

"That was the person we're looking for," I said. "Whoever it was tried to steal Tiffany's surfboard."

Ashley picked up the board. The pink paint and black marker had been cleaned away. It looked almost brand new.

"Wow," I said. "Why does Tiffany need to win a surfboard in a contest when she's got this? I wish I had a board this nice."

"Maybe she just likes to win," Ashley suggested. "She does have a lot of medals."

"Well, we'd better take this back to her," I said.

We carried the board to Tiffany's cabin. Lights glowed through the windows. Good. Somebody must be there.

I propped the board against the wall and knocked.

For a second I thought I saw somebody peeking out from behind the curtains. But no one answered the door.

I knocked again. Still no answer.

"Is it okay to just leave the board here?" Ashley asked.

"I don't know." I looked around. "Maybe we can hide it somewhere."

I started to move the board, when the door opened.

"Hi, guys. What's up?" Tiffany stood in the doorway, wearing a fluffy white bathrobe.

So she was home all along. *How come she didn't answer the door sooner?* I wondered.

"I thought I heard somebody knocking," she said with a laugh. "I was just taking a shower."

Oh. That explained it.

We told Tiffany about how someone tried to steal her surfboard.

She stared at the board with a terrible expression on her face. "Who is doing this to me?" Tears glistened in her eyes. "I never want to see that stupid surfboard again!"

*Wow*, I thought. *She's really upset!*

"I know you guys are doing everything you can to help me." Tiffany sighed. "But it's no use. Maybe you should just forget about this case. I don't want to ruin your whole vacation."

She carried her surfboard inside.

My shoulders slumped. I felt terrible. Was Tiffany right? Had we finally found a mystery we couldn't solve?

I glanced at Ashley. But she didn't look sad at all. She had that look on her face. The one she always gets when she's trying to figure something out.

"What's up?" I whispered.

Ashley tilted her head. "Did you see the purple bathing suit strap sticking out of Tiffany's bathrobe?"

"What?" I exclaimed. "No way. That doesn't make any sense."

"I know," Ashley agreed. "But I'm sure I saw it. Why would Tiffany take a shower with her bathing suit on?"

"That would be weird," I agreed. "Do you think she was lying about taking a shower?"

"Maybe. And if she just took a shower, why wasn't her hair wet?" Ashley said. "Mine always gets soaked."

"Well, maybe she wore a shower cap," I suggested.

"Maybe," Ashley said slowly. "But I still think something weird is going on."

"Let's ask Tiffany when she comes back," I said.

We waited. Ashley tapped her foot. Clue sniffed the doormat. I glanced at my watch.

Oh, no!

"We don't have time to wait for her," I told Ashley. "It's eight fifty-five. Jazz is supposed to get paid in five minutes. If we

don't hurry over to the Eat-Here Hut, we'll miss it!"

"Bye, Tiffany!" I shouted in through the doorway. "We've got to go!"

With Clue leading the way, we ran all the way to the Eat-Here Hut. Then we hid behind one of the giant palm trees in the parking lot. It was a good hiding place. It had a great view of the restaurant.

A minute later someone holding an envelope appeared. The person was wearing a baseball cap. I couldn't tell who it was.

"Let's get him—or her," I said.

"No," Ashley whispered. "Not yet."

We watched the person place the envelope on the ground next to the restaurant. Then we jumped out and rushed forward. Our suspect just stood there, too shocked to move.

But when we saw who it was, *we* were the ones who were shocked!

## 11

# MARY-KATE HAS A HUNCH

"**J**ennifer!" I cried.

I was totally surprised.

Ashley looked amazed, too. "Why?" she asked Jennifer. "Why are you doing this?"

"I know why," I broke in. "You really like Scott. You messed up Tiffany's board to help him!"

Jennifer shook her head. She looked scared. "I didn't! I mean, I do, but I didn't!"

Ashley pulled out her notebook. "Could you repeat that, please?" she asked.

Jennifer sighed. "I *do* like Scott," she admitted. "But I did *not* touch Tiffany's surfboard. I promise!"

"We can't prove you did anything wrong," Ashley said.

"But you have to admit you seem kind of guilty." I pointed to the envelope.

"I can prove I didn't do anything bad to Tiffany!" Jennifer said. "I like Tiffany. I'm doing her a favor right now by dropping off this envelope. She asked me to!"

Ashley and I glanced at each other.

I was confused. If Tiffany asked Jennifer to deliver the money, that meant Tiffany was paying Jazz.

And *that* meant Tiffany told Jazz to scare her with the shark toy. She was scaring herself on purpose. Could it really be true?

"Okay, we believe you," I said quickly.

Ashley looked at me as if I were nuts.

"Trust me," I whispered to her.

"You can go," I told Jennifer. "As long as you give us the envelope."

"Thanks, guys," Jennifer said. Then she was gone.

Ashley and I opened the envelope. Inside we found a five-dollar bill. There was also a note that said: YOU MESSED UP, SO YOU ONLY GET HALF!

"Ashley," I said. "This handwriting matches both the other notes. I'm absolutely sure of it."

"I think so, too," Ashley agreed. "But we still don't know for sure if Tiffany wrote it."

Just then Jazz rode by on his bike. He leaned over and snatched the envelope from my hand. Then he raced off down the street.

"There goes our evidence," Ashley said.

"Don't worry," I told her. "We don't need it. I'm sure Tiffany is the one who pulled all these pranks." We headed back to the resort. "But I still don't know why."

"How do you know Jennifer isn't lying?" Ashley said. "She could have written all three notes—and that's why they match."

"I have a hunch," I said.

Ashley squinted. "Mary-Kate..."

"Jennifer is a really bad speller," I told her. "And all three notes were spelled perfectly. I don't think she wrote them."

"What about the note on the surfboard—when Tiffany's name was spelled wrong?" Ashley asked.

"I think Tiffany did that on purpose," I told her. "To trick us so we wouldn't figure out the mystery."

"But why would Tiffany want to scare herself?" Ashley asked. "It doesn't make sense. We need to find out her motive. And we need proof that she did it."

I thought about that as we walked Clue back to our room. But when we passed the swimming pool, I knew I didn't need anything more.

"There's your proof," I said, pointing.

It was Tiffany.

She was wobbling on her surfboard—trying really hard to do a single pop-up.

In the baby pool!

## 12

# CASE CLOSED— WITH A SPLASH

$A$shley and I crept closer. We tried not to make a sound.

"Shh!" I whispered to Clue.

We watched Tiffany standing on the fancy, expensive surfboard in the smooth water of the baby pool.

And then she did something really surprising.

She fell off the board. *Splash!*

She looked as if she had never been on a surfboard in her life!

"Mary-Kate," Ashley whispered. "Are you thinking what I'm thinking?"

I nodded. "Tiffany's not a top surfer. She doesn't know how to surf at all."

Ashley and I stepped from the shadows and walked to the edge of the tiny pool.

"Hi, Tiffany," I said.

Tiffany gasped. "Uh, h-hi, guys." She smiled crookedly. "I, uh—" She tried to laugh. "You see, I was just kind of fooling around here, you know…"

Tiffany climbed out of the pool. She wrapped a beach towel around her shoulders. Then we all sat on some deck chairs.

Ashley and I didn't speak. Great-grandma Olive taught us that, too. Sometimes if you don't say anything, your suspect will think you know everything.

"I guess you guys really are super detectives after all," Tiffany said quietly. "You finally figured out who's been trying to scare me."

We waited, our eyes on her.

"What?" Tiffany asked. "Why are you looking at me like that?"

We didn't say a word.

Tiffany shifted in her seat. She glanced at the baby pool. Then she looked at us. "You know, don't you?" she said. "You know I did everything to myself."

Mystery solved. I was right. But for once I didn't feel like cheering.

"Mary-Kate figured that part out," Ashley told her. "And now it all makes sense. Nobody stole your board tonight. It was you we saw, right?"

Tiffany nodded. "I was on my way here to practice pop-ups. I didn't think there would be anybody around this late."

"But there's one thing we *don't* understand," I said.

"What?" Tiffany asked, not looking at either of us.

"Why did you do it?" I asked her.

Tiffany shrugged. "I…" She looked as if she might be trying to make up an excuse. But then she shook her head. "I'm afraid of the ocean!"

Huh? This was the last thing we expected to hear!

"I don't get it," I said.

Tiffany wrapped the beach towel closer around her shoulders. "It's true," she said. "I don't ever want to go in the water."

"But you're a champion swimmer!" Ashley protested. "What about all your medals! How did you win them if you don't like to go swimming?"

"I didn't say I don't like to swim," Tiffany replied. "I love it. I said I hate the *ocean*. I won all my medals in a swimming pool."

"But what's the big deal?" Ashley asked her. "Why sign up for surfing lessons and the contest in the first place?"

"It's my parents," Tiffany explained. "Especially my dad. He always wanted me

to surf because he loves the ocean so much. He learned to surf when he was a kid. When he got older, he won lots of surfing championships."

"Did he ever take you surfing?" I wanted to know.

"I grew up in Ohio," Tiffany explained. "There's no beach there. My dad doesn't even know that I'm afraid of the ocean."

She shivered. "One time when I was really little, my dad took me to the beach in Hawaii. I was scared of the big waves. Daddy told me not to be afraid. But then he let go—and a gigantic wave knocked me down."

Tiffany buried her face in her hands. "I was scared the crabs would pinch my toes," she said. "I was scared a shark might eat me. I was scared of everything!"

Ashley patted her shoulder.

"Dad heard about the junior surfing contest. He thought I would have fun if I took a

few lessons and entered the contest," Tiffany said. "But I was too chicken to even try it."

I was beginning to understand Tiffany's problem and why she pulled the pranks on herself.

"My dad wants me to be a champion surfer like he was," she went on. "And my parents always say that I can be the best at anything." Tears began to trickle down her cheeks. "They expect me to win the contest tomorrow. But I can't even enter it. I'm too scared to go in the water."

"So you tried to make it look as if someone was scaring you," Ashley said. "That way you had an excuse to stay out of the contest."

Tiffany nodded. "Now what am I going to do?"

"Just tell your parents the truth," Ashley said.

"I can't!" Tiffany protested.

"Sure you can," I told her. "I saw your parents. They're really proud of you. I know they must love you very much."

Tiffany wiped her eyes on her beach towel. "You're right. I will. And guys? I'm really sorry. About everything."

"That's okay," I told her. "We understand."

Then Tiffany smiled for the first time that evening. "I knew you two were great detectives! That's why I gave you that creepy note. I wanted to scare you off before you found out the truth. But nothing scares you two. You're the best."

Ashley and I slapped each other five.

We cracked another case!

The next morning everyone at the resort gathered on the beach for the big surfing contest.

Ashley and I looked around for Tiffany.

She was standing next to her mom and

dad. They looked happy. When I waved, Tiffany ran over.

"I told my parents everything," she told us. "And guess what? They said *they* were sorry for making me feel like I had to be the best at everything. They just want me to be me."

"So everything's okay?" Ashley said.

"Well, not exactly," Tiffany admitted. "I'm grounded for everything I did. But I can't blame them."

"Are you going to watch us surf?" I asked.

"I wouldn't miss it!" Tiffany said. "I want to see if you guys are as good at surfing as you are at solving mysteries!"

Ashley and I did our best, and we had a great time.

Scott won first place. Jennifer cheered like crazy, of course.

T.J. came in second. I guess he was almost as good as he thought he was!

And Ashley and I tied for third.

You'll never guess what we won.

Another round of surfing lessons for next year.

We can't wait!

*Hi from the both of us,*

It all started when Princess Patty dared us to spend half an hour in a haunted house. It was creepy, but we almost made it—until we saw a ghost!

Was someone trying to trick us, or was the house really haunted? We had to find out— or give Patty our Halloween candy!

But that wasn't our only mystery. All our friends were building sculptures out of Popsicle sticks for a contest. Then somebody started stealing all the sticks in town! We had to find the thief fast—before the contest was ruined.

To read more about our spooky case, turn the page for a sneak peek at our newest adventure: *The Case of the Green Ghost.*

See you next time!

*Love,*

*Ashley Olsen* & *Mary-Kate Olsen*

# The Case Of The
# Green Ghost™

"There it is," Patty O'Leary said in a spooky voice. "The old Bennett house—the one I told you about in my ghost story. I heard the last family who lived there had to move out because the ghost wouldn't leave them alone."

My heart beat faster as I stared at the big, old house. It was totally dark. Some of the windows had boards over them. The chimney was black and crooked. The front steps sagged and there were cobwebs across the door.

Was there really a ghost in there?

"I bet there are bats inside," Tim murmured. "Did you ever see any, Jeremy?"

Jeremy nodded. He lives next door. "Yeah, and I've heard a spooky wailing noise lots of times," he said.

"It's the ghost," Patty declared.

Ashley shook her head. "No way. There's no such thing as ghosts! It's just the wind in the chimney."

Samantha shivered. "Well, I wouldn't want to go inside that place, especially at night."

"It's just an old house," Ashley told her. "There's nothing to be scared of."

"Mary-Kate is scared," Patty said with a laugh. "Look at her—she's shivering!"

"I'm just cold," I snapped.

"Mary-Kate isn't scared," Ashley told her. "And neither am I."

"Okay, if you're so brave, why don't you just go in there?" Patty demanded. "Go on. See if you can stay there for a whole half hour. I dare you!"

What? No way was I going in that house!

I don't know if ghosts are real or not—but I didn't want to find out the hard way!

But before I could say anything, Ashley spoke up.

"Okay, we'll do it!" Ashley declared. "We'll *prove* there aren't any ghosts. Right, Mary-Kate?"

Oh, no! How could Ashley do this to me?

"Right, Mary-Kate?" Ashley repeated.

I *really* didn't want to go into that house. But I had to back Ashley up. "Uh…right," I agreed.

"You'll be sorrrry!" Patty said in a sing-song voice. "Especially when you lose. Because whoever loses has to give the winner their Halloween candy. *All* of it!"

"Fine. Except you're the one who's going to be sorry," Ashley told her. "Come on, Mary-Kate."

"No, don't!" Jeremy stepped in front of us. "Listen, you guys," he said. "The place really *is* haunted. I should know—I live next door. I hear that wailing noise all the time. And moaning sounds, too. There's a really *bad* ghost in there. You can't go in!"

Uh-oh. Now I really, *really* didn't want to go into the house!

"Um, well—we better not, Ashley," I said. I glanced up at the sky. "It's getting dark."

"You *are* scared!" Patty sneered.

"No, we're not," Ashley said. "But Mary-Kate's right. We don't have enough time. We have to be home before dark."

*Whew!* I thought. *Saved!*

Then Ashley added, "We'll just do it tomorrow."

*Noooo!*

Patty frowned. "Okay, I guess," she grumbled. "But you have to do it first thing in the morning. It's Saturday—there's no school. We'll meet here at nine o'clock sharp."

"You guys don't know what you're getting into," Jeremy warned Ashley and me. "Messing with a ghost could be dangerous. Don't do it!"

"We have to," Ashley told him.

Jeremy shuddered. "Well, I'm not going to come and watch."

"I *can't* come," Zach said. "I have to go shopping with my Mom. What a drag!"

"Don't worry," Patty told him. "When Mary-Kate and Ashley run into the ghost, you'll be able to hear them screaming all over town!"

The next morning, when Ashley and I walked up to the Bennett house, Patty, Samantha and Tim were waiting for us.

"Are you ready?" Patty asked.

"We can't wait," Ashley told her.

I looked at the house. Even in the bright sunshine, it was creepy.

*I can wait*, I thought.

But Ashley was already marching up the

sidewalk to the front steps.

I took a deep breath and followed her.

"Good luck!" Samantha called.

"You won't last ten minutes!" Patty added.

Ashley and I walked up to the front door. "Let's get this over with," I said.

"Don't worry," Ashley told me. "There isn't any ghost in there—and we're going to prove it. Ready?"

I swallowed hard. "Ready," I said.

Ashley turned the door handle and pushed.

*Creaak!* Shivers ran up my spine as the door slowly opened. We stepped inside.

*Creaak!* The door swung shut—by itself!

Heavy red velvet curtains covered the windows. It was dark inside. Dark and cold.

"Do you hear anything?" Ashley whispered.

"No! What?" I asked. "What did you hear?"

"I thought I heard a noise," she replied. "Kind of a rustling. It could have been a squirrel or something."

Ashley sounded a little nervous. That made me even *more* nervous.

We took out our flashlights and turned them on. I glanced around. We were standing in a huge hall with a wide, curved staircase on one side. Strips of wallpaper curled down to the floor. Thousands of cobwebs hung from the walls and ceiling.

Suddenly, *I* heard the rustling noise. Then a bat swooped down from the ceiling!

"Ashley, look out!" I cried.

We both ducked. I threw my arms up to protect my head.

The bat swept over our heads. It fluttered up the stairway to the second floor.

"Whoa!" Ashley gasped. "That was close!"

"Let's get out of here, now!" I said.

"No! We can't quit yet, Mary-Kate," Ashley argued. "We have to stay here for half an hour. Do you want to lose the bet and give Patty all your Halloween candy?"

"No, but..."

"And it's not just the candy," Ashley said. "She'll call us wimps for the rest of our lives."

I sighed. Ashley was right. "Okay," I said. "But if a bat gets in my hair, I'm out of here. I mean it!"

We walked toward the staircase. Ashley stopped at the bottom of the stairs. She shined her light on the floor. "Look."

I glanced down. Drops of green, gooey-looking stuff were spattered near the bottom stair.

"Weird," I said. I bent down to check it out.

"Listen!" Ashley grabbed my arm. "What's that noise?"

I froze. My heart pounded like crazy as I listened.

*Swoosh...swoosh...swoosh.*

A shuffling sound was coming from the second floor. We shined our flashlights up the staircase.

*Swoosh...Swoosh...*

A shape suddenly appeared at the top of the stairs. A ghostly shape, green and shimmering. I gasped. It didn't have a head!

It hovered there for a second, swaying back and forth.

Then...SWOOSH! It swooped down the stairs, heading straight at Ashley and me!

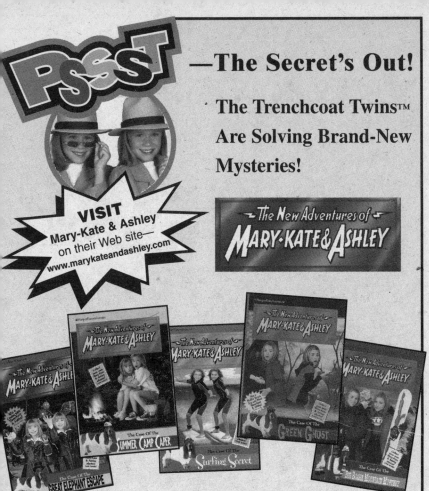
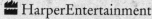

# Surf's Up!

## Win A Malibu Beach Trip
### and meet
# Mary-Kate & Ashley!

*You're invited to Mary-Kate & Ashley's Hawaiian Beach Party™ video for*
**100 FIRST PRIZE WINNERS!**

**Grand Prize Winner** will also receive a totally cool surfboard autographed by Mary-Kate & Ashley

---

## Complete this entry form and send it to:

The New Adventures of Mary-Kate & Ashley™ Malibu Beach Sweepstakes
c/o HarperCollins Publishers
Attn: Department AW-Malibu
10 East 53rd Street
New York, NY 10022

No purchase necessary. See details on back.

Visit our website at
www.marykateandashley.com

Name: _____

Address: _____

City: _____ State:_____ Zip: _____

Phone: _____ Age: _____

---

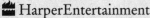

**HarperEntertainment**
*A Division of HarperCollinsPublishers*
www.harpercollins.com

The New Adventures of
Mary-Kate & Ashley
TM & © 1999 Dualstar
Entertainment Group, Inc.

PARACHUTE PRESS

**DUALSTAR** PUBLICATIONS

## OFFICIAL RULES

1. No purchase necessary.

2. To enter complete the official entry form or hand print your name, address, and phone number along with the words "The New Adventures of Mary-Kate & Ashley™ Malibu Beach Sweepstakes" on a 3 x 5 card and mail to: The New Adventures of Mary-Kate & Ashley™ / Malibu Beach Sweepstakes c/o HarperCollins Publishers Attn: Department AW-Malibu, 10 East 53rd Street, New York, NY 10022. All entries must be postmarked no later than December 31, 1999. Enter as often as you wish, but each entry must be mailed separately. One entry per envelope. Partially completed, illegible or mechanically reproduced entries will not be accepted. Sponsors are not responsible for lost, late, mutilated, illegible, stolen, postage due, incomplete or misdirected entries. All entries become the property of Dualstar Entertainment Group, Inc., and will not be returned.

3. Sweepstakes open to all legal residents of the United States, who are between the ages of five and twelve by December 31, 1999 excluding employees and immediate family members of HarperCollins, Parachute Properties and Parachute Press, Inc., and their respective subsidiaries and affiliates, officers, directors, shareholders, employees, agents, attorneys and other representatives (individually and collectively "Parachute"), Dualstar Entertainment Group, Inc. and its subsidiaries and affiliates, officers, directors, shareholders, employees, agents, attorneys and other representatives (individually and collectively "Dualstar"), and their respective parent companies, affiliates, subsidiaries, advertising, promotion and fulfillment agencies, and the persons with whom each of the above are domiciled. Offer void where prohibited or restricted.

4. Odds of winning depend on total number of entries received. All prizes will be awarded. Winners will be randomly drawn on or about January 14, 2000 by HarperCollins Publishers whose decisions are final. Potential winner will be notified by mail and potential winner will be required to sign and return an affidavit of eligibility and release of liability within 14 days of notification, or another winner will be chosen. Prizes won by minors will be awarded to parent or legal guardian who must sign and return all required legal documents. By acceptance of the prize, winner consents to the use of his/her name, photograph, likeness, and personal information by HarperCollins, Parachute, and Dualstar, for publicity purposes without further compensation except where prohibited.

5. One (1) Grand Prize Winner will win a trip to Malibu Beach and the chance to meet Mary-Kate and Ashley Olsen. The Grand Prize Winner will also receive a surf board autographed by Mary-Kate and Ashley. HarperCollins, Parachute, and Dualstar, reserve the right to substitute another prize of equal or greater value in the event that the winner is unable to receive the prize for any reason. All expenses not stated are at the winner's sole expense. (Total approximate value:$3,200.00). 100 First Prize Winners will receive a copy of *You're Invited to Mary-Kate & Ashley's Hawaiian Beach Party* video (Total approximate value $12.95 each).

5a. HarperCollins Publishers will provide the contest winner and a) [two parents] or b) [a legal guardian and a second child] with round-trip air transportation from major airport nearest winner to Los Angeles, standard hotel accommodations for a two night stay, an autographed surf board, and the chance to meet Mary-Kate and Ashley Olsen, subject to availability. Trip must be taken within one year from the date prize is awarded. All additional expenses including taxes, meals, gratuities, and incidentals are the responsibility of the prize winner. Airline, accommodation and other travel arrangements will be made by HarperCollins in its discretion. HarperCollins reserves the right to substitute a cash payment of equal value for the Grand Prize. Travel and use of accommodation are at risk of winner and HarperCollins does not assume any liability.

6. Only one prize will be awarded per individual, family, or household. Prizes are non-transferable and cannot be sold or redeemed for cash. Any federal, state, or local taxes are the responsibility of the winner.

7. Additional terms: By participating, entrants agree a) to the official rules and decisions of the judges which will be final in all respects; and b) to release, discharge and hold harmless HarperCollins, Parachute, Dualstar, and their affiliates, subsidiaries and advertising and promotion agencies from and against any and all liability or damages associated with acceptance, use or misuse of any prize received in this sweepstakes.

8. To obtain the name of the winner, please send your request and a self-addressed stamped envelope (excluding residents of Vermont and Washington) to The New Adventures of Mary-Kate & Ashley™ Malibu Beach Sweepstakes, c/o HarperEntertainment, 10 East 53rd Street, New York, NY, 10022.

# PARTY IN STYLE

## WITH MARY-KATE AND ASHLEY!

You'll go Simply Wild for Their All New Video.

YOU'RE INVITED TO **MARY-KATE & ASHLEY'S**™
FASHION PARTY™

Each Video includes a Mary-Kate and Ashley Sampler book from Harper Entertainment.

Own it on video this fall.

DUALSTAR VIDEO

KidVision
A DIVISION OF
WARNERVISION
ENTERTAINMENT

# High Above Hollywood
# Mary-Kate & Ashley Are Playing
# Matchmakers!
## Check Them Out in Their Coolest New Movie

**Mary-Kate**
**Olsen**

**Ashley**
**Olsen**

# Billboard DAD

One's a surfer. The other's a high diver. When these two team up to find a new love for their single Dad by taking out a personals ad on a billboard in the heart of Hollywood, it's a fun-loving, eye-catching California adventure gone wild!

# Now on Video!

DUALSTAR
VIDEO

**Load up
the one horse
open sleigh.
Mary-Kate and Ashley's
Christmas Album
is on the way.**

It doesn't matter if you live around the corner...
or around the world....
If you are a fan of Mary-Kate and Ashley Olsen,
you should be a member of

# Mary-Kate + Ashley's Fun Club™

Here's what you get
Our Funzine™
An autographed color photo
Two black and white individual photos
A full sized color poster
An official Fun Club™ membership card
A Fun Club™ School folder
Two special Fun Club™ surprises
Fun Club™ Collectible Catalog
Plus a Fun Club™ box to keep everything in.

To join Mary-Kate + Ashley's Fun Club™, fill out the form below
and send it along with

| | |
|---|---|
| U.S. Residents | $17.00 |
| Canadian Residents | $22.00 (US Funds only) |
| International Residents | $27.00 (US Funds only) |

## Mary-Kate + Ashley's Fun Club™
## 859 Hollywood Way, Suite 275
## Burbank, CA 91505

Name:_____

Address:_____

City:_____ St:_____ Zip:_____

Phone: (_____) _____

E-Mail:_____

Check us out on the web at
# www.marykateandashley.com